William Brown

The Commercial Crisis, its Cause and Cure

SALZWASSER
VERLAG

.

William Brown

The Commercial Crisis, its Cause and Cure

Reprint of the original.

1st Edition 2023 | ISBN: 978-3-37514-646-7

Verlag (Publisher): Salzwasser Verlag GmbH, Zeilweg 44, 60439 Frankfurt, Deutschland
Vertretungsberechtigt (Authorized to represent): E. Roepke, Zeilweg 44, 60439 Frankfurt, Deutschland
Druck (Print): Books on Demand GmbH, In de Tarpen 42, 22848 Norderstedt, Deutschland

THE

COMMERCIAL CRISIS;

ITS CAUSE AND CURE.

TWO LECTURES

DELIVERED IN BONAVENTURE HALL, MONTREAL, ON THE 30th
DECEMBER, 1857, AND 4th FEBRUARY, 1858,

BY

WILLIAM BROWN,

COTE-DES-NEIGES NURSERIES, NEAR MONTREAL.

MONTREAL:
SALTER & ROSS, PRINTERS, GREAT ST. JAMES STREET.

1858

FIRST LECTURE.

DELIVERED 30th DEC. 1857.—T. S. BROWN, ESQ. IN THE CHAIR.

The subject of our present lecture is " THE COMMERCIAL CRISIS—
ITS CAUSE AND CURE." The matter is one of such vast importance,
embracing all classes of the community, and affecting such various pas-
sions and interests, that I cannot approach it but with extreme diffi-
dence. The gravity of the subject demands from my audience a patient hearing. You have all an individual interest in the matter ; and
not only is the welfare of your families, your servants, your neighbors,
your ministers, your country, all concerned—but it involves the welfare
of the kingdom of Christ, of the church of God. The views which I
will advance will be to many, if not most of you, so new, and apparently
so much at variance with your pecuniary interests, and altogether so an-
tagonistic to " the course of this world," that I cannot expect at once to
gain people over to my views. But if, as I believe, these views are
founded on truth and correct principles, this lecture will not have been
delivered in vain. Should I succeed in inducing but a few of you to
examine into the matter for yourselves, laying aside all preconceived
notions, and being guided solely by Divine revelation and your own reasons, I shall feel well satisfied. I would not wish to force my opinions
upon any one ; I only desire in a calm and quiet manner to lay them out
before your minds, so that you may bring your own reflective faculties
to bear upon them, and thus let every one be convinced in his own mind.
I have myself held these views for a considerable period ; and the tre-
mendous commercial convulsion, or panic, or distress, or whatever else
you may please to call it, through which we are now passing, has only
tended to strengthen and confirm them. I may say here, without wish-
ing to reflect at all on the character or intelligence of this meeting, that
I will expect hereafter to be met with all sorts of arguments, many of
them quite foreign to the subject, or put in a captious spirit. Such arguments I will of course take no notice of, but if any should come for-

ward in a spirit of brotherly love, and for the sake of eliciting the truth, on which ever side it may be found, I trust I will be ready to meet him in the same spirit.

I believe in a Divine over-ruling Providence—that God made man upright, after his own image, but that he hath sought out many inventions, and sadly defaced that beautiful image. I believe, moreover, that all things happen according to his omniscient decree, whether it be an Indian mutiny, or the burning of a " Montreal" steamship, the destruction of a Sodom, or the fall of a sparrow. It is one of the tendencies of this age in which we live—in fact, I think, its prevailing and besetting sin—to get rid of the *idea of God* altogether. It will not permit Him to have any hand in the government of that world which He created for His own glory, and which He preserves by His almighty power until the consummation of all things. The events which are daily taking place in our midst, whether for good or evil—the frequent and appalling accidents which are continually occurring, and which no human foresight seems sufficient to guard against—the horrors of war, or the march of the pestilence through the land—all are ascribed to chance, or to some other of the vain imaginations of the heart of man ; and so we see, throughout all the world, mankind in his wickedness and folly, and for the sake of worldly gain, making a speculation of the most sacred things and the most solemn events, even of death itself—that change which awaits us all, and against which no insurance can guard. Depend upon it, there are more gaming tables amongst us than those frequented by the ordinary gambler, not the less hateful in the sight of God, which the conventionalities of our apologetic system have clothed in a dress at once lawful and respectable. If there are some things amongst us so loathsome that they ought not to be so much as named, there are others so sacred that they should be preserved from the contamination of a worldly and hoarding spirit.

And as with the providence or government of God in the world, so with the book which He has written to be a guide to that world in all circumstances and throughout all time. If any of its Divine precepts are to be admitted, the New Testament portion of it is deemed sufficient for the wants of mankind now, or rather for the extent and aggravation of his sins, as if the hoar antiquity of the Old Testament, with all its rugged and sublime truths, was out of place amidst the genteel and polished morality of our later age. There is as much danger of taking away from, as adding to, the words of the book of prophecy; and accordingly we find its promises and its threatenings, its glorious imagery and its artless stories, its incidents of love, zeal, truth, holiness and faith—all dying away in a solemn warning against that presumption and infatuation which the Spirit of God foresaw would lead man to be wise in his own conceit, and induce him to mutilate and pervert that book which is an embodiment of everything that is divine and holy. And this leads me to reflect that no new truth will ever be enunciated to this world. God has deemed the Bible sufficient for the wants of man in whatever position or relationship he may be placed, whether as individuals or communities; and the further we go from its divine precepts and maxims, the more sorrow and wretchedness we experience, for an infallible decree has been pronounced that sin shall ever be conjoined with suffering. And this leads me further to say, that if there are any who hear me to-night who consider that the requirements of the present age have out-run the simple truths of Scripture, my arguments will in all likelihood be heard by them in vain. I intend, in short, to base these arguments upon the Bible, especially the ancient portion of it, and to endeavor to shew that it is in consequence of our departure from its wise and holy commandments—our non-conformity with its simple precepts—that so much sorrow and suffering at present exist amongst us. I cannot conceal from you that it is with feelings of awe and solemnity that I approach this momentous subject, for I may, perhaps, be laying my feeble hands on a lever so mighty as to move a world, on a spring whose echo may yet, in the far future, resound from shore to shore. To the reason and intellegence of all unprejudiced minds I appeal. "Judge ye what I say."

We are at present, as a nation, in the furnace of affliction. Two dire calamities have befallen us. The Indian mutiny and the commercial crisis, synchronical as they are in period, have attracted the minds of all, and they will both, no doubt, be seen in their results for many years to come. Whilst the mutiny, in its more immediate effects, is as yet confined to British India, the commercial convulsion has shaken every civilized nation to its centre, and a period of prostration is now alloted to us, such, perhaps, as has never before been experienced. It ought to be a matter of the deepest thankfulness to every lover of his country, that Great Britain, in this Indian mutiny, has, as a nation, humbled herself in the sight of Almighty God on account of her sins; nor can we tell how much this humiliation and national repentance has had to do with the glorious successes which have recently attended our arms; or with the indomitable courage and heroism which have made the names of a Havelock and a Nicholson household words, and called forth at once the wonder and admiration of the world. The empire, so far as circumstances at present permit us to judge, seems to have rightly appreciated and acted up to her true position; and although many once happy families will long mourn the desolating effects of the great mutiny over their vacant hearths and blighted homes; although there can be no doubt we have been compelled to drink the bitter cup of our own mixing, yet it is most consolitory to think, that out of it all, has come a national humiliation, and a national desire now to do our duty to the perishing millions under our sway.

But whilst, in certain aspects, it is consolitory and refreshing thus to contemplate the Indian mutiny and its effects, it is sad to think that a commercial period of unprecedented distress has fallen upon us, which will, to all appearance, depart just as other and similar trials have departed, and that the community will again, whenever opportunity occurs, rush along in the same suicidal course. The great wave of commerce will again swell and carry on its breast many a joyous heart; soon it will burst with its usual destructive power, and subside as others have subsided before it, leaving nothing behind but broken wrecks and ruined hopes. These convulsions have now become periodical; and, moreover, they seem to come not only with renewed vigor, but with increasing swiftness. All suffer by these visitations more or less. Thousands who had held stations of affluence and respectability are brought down to bankruptcy and ruin; stocks fall to an alarming extent; the resources of the government are crippled to a degree inimical to the safety of the country; fearful anxiety is in every eye, fever in every heart, and trembling on every tongue; money is withdrawn through fear and panic from its proper and lawful circulation; some, rather than meet the dishonor of bankruptcy, fill an untimely grave; the poor, virtuous as well as vicious, are thrown out of employment, and then comes *poverty* in its desperation and wretchedness to haunt our streets and lanes; crime increases on every side; our jails are filled with the vicious, and perhaps too often with those who are compelled to steal to support their famishing bodies; the honest creditor begs in vain for his just debt, the honest workman for work, the hungry child for a morsel of meat; troops are collected to guard state treasure ; the cause of gospel missions languishes ; the progress of science and art is arrested ; banks are reduced to the ignominy (for we can call it by no milder name) of refusing to redeem their own notes—many of them, heretofore considered the safest of institutions, burst on every side ; a wide door is opened for dissimulation, crime, and fraud of every dye. In short, we behold the spectacle of a whole civilized world groaning and travailing together in pain ! And as commerce multiplies its agents and extends its bounds, the evil increases, the danger becomes more imminent, and the effects more enduring. The cloud which arose in America, speedily spreads and covers the horizon of Europe. From that continent, and, sad to think, principally from that nation we call the first in the world for wealth and intelligence, we hear of nothing but commercial tumult and disorder.

Then if you come to enquire into the cause of these troubles, you will find reasons given as various as the clouds, as opposite as the poles. One will tell you that it arises from the speculation in land—another from overtrading—another from the stringency of the banks (for the banks, like government, I perceive, are considered to have broad shoulders, and many are the sins they have to answer for if all is true that is laid to their doors)—another will tell you it arises from the errors or corruptions of the government—another will lay it to the charge of our friends across the line—another to the absorption of capital by railroads —another to the giving of reckless credit—another to the absence of banking capital—and another to people not paying their debts—and so on. Thus apparently all are in uncertainty and doubt. With most, the relief from stringency to relaxation—from darkness to light—is found to be only a question of time ; and time does, indeed, always work a certain kind of cure, simply, I suppose, because all have gone down who were too weak to buffet with the stream. Instead of enquiring into the principles which lay at the root of all commercial transactions, or into the propriety, consistency and mo ality of those rules which have been laid down as our unerring and safest guides in matters between man and man, we find each one striving to throw the blame on his neighbor, when, in fact, as all are involved in the common ruin, all, through the error of their ways, are more or less guilty of bringing that ruin upon their own heads. Never, to me, has a plainer question been involved by mankind in general in more obscurity ; never have plainer truths been more completely darkened by words without reason than those which are intended by the Divine author of our being to be guides to us in the common transactions of life. The system of our commercial relationship and transactions one with another, has become so venerable from the dust of years, so completely embraces all interests and classes of the community, and has become so thoroughly incorporated with everything political, social and sacred, that, to the eye of sense, it looks as if no change could ever take place in the monstrous system. We know, however, that a change must take place—that a little leaven of truth, will, in the end, leaven the whole lump—that mankind will not always submit to a system fertile only in ruin, degradation and sorrow. Influences are at work which must, in their very nature, bring to an end not only that despotism and tyranny under which mankind have so long groaned, but also the corruptions which sway every department of our social being, as well as the errors of a misguided commerce. We will not always suffer shadow for substance—pretension for fact. Agencies are at work, which will eventually overturn the present state of things, and be the means of bringing in a period when all the world will be vocal with His praise.

Time warns me, however, to proceed to the subject now immediately upon our thoughts.

It pleased God in the counsels of eternity, to select from all the nations of the earth, one upon whom He would bestow distinguished privileges and unheard of glory. It was fitting that that interesting and ancient race, out of whose loins sprung our blessed Lord himself, should be distinguished in every respect from all other nations—should stand forth to all time, at once a memorial of His love, and a memento of His worth. A glory encircles the brow of ancient Israel, compared with which the splendor of a Persian monarchy—the learning of a Grecian—the renown of a Roman—or the commercial greatness of our own—are as but the dross compared to the fine gold. A halo rests upon her tomb, the promise of a future and glorious resurrection. And as into this holy casket were dropped jewels of priceless worth, so out of it came character of inestimable value. To this people was committed the whole law of God. The *ceremonial* portion of it—that which shadowed forth in *ceremonial observances,*—the person, offices and work of Christ—has been done away with. When he who was the great substance came, there was no further need of those things which had shadowed him forth. Men have no need of a candle in the blaze of day. But the moral and judicial or civil law of God is something in itself indestructible as the ever-lasting hills, fitted for all races and tongues and for all time. By the moral law I mean simply those things which God hath told us are right, and those which he hath told us are wrong, and however this fanciful age may delight to call things wrong which are right, and things right which are wrong, yet they are, in themselves, like God himself, the same yester-day, to-day, and for ever, and the most subtle arguments of the most subtle minds can never change their nature or character. And that these laws, enunciated by those " holy men of old who spoke as they were moved by the Holy Ghost," are yet binding on the hearts and con-sciences of men, we have the most incontestible evidence from Christ himself, who tells us that he came, not to destroy, but to fulfil the law and the prophets. " We have Moses and the prophets, let us hear them." Now I know it has become the fashion to consider that many of the divine laws promulgated in the Old Testament have been done away with by the milder spirit of the New—that an eye for an eye and a tooth for a tooth, has now no place in the economy of the Gospel—an idea as repugnant to the most superficial interpretation of Scripture as it is to common sense. It is another common error, and the fruitful source of much immorality, that many of the Mosaic laws were intended for a Mosaic period—that they were never suited for the increasing intelligence, and abounding commerce, and expanding views of the present age. But how will this agree with the declaration of Christ that not one tittle of his law shall fail or pass away? How can it agree with the fact that the same sins which are committed now, were com-mitted then? That the heart of man, now as ever, is deceitful above all things and desperately wicked? Every part of the law of God, pro-fitable and needed then, is profitable and needed now ; for *all* Scripture is given by inspiration of God, and is profitable for doctrine and reproof, instruction and correction He who knows the hearts of all men, and saw the end from the beginning, provided a law binding on the earliest and latest ages, and suited for all men and all time. There are problems, commercial and political, yet to be solved, connected with the history of Israel, of which the world has not yet dreamed.

The sin in our commercial transactions to which I would this evening more particularly direct your attention, is that of giving forth money upon usury, or as the word in the original means, " increase," or as it is com-monly used in our day, " on interest." We have abundance of proof,

from the Scriptures themselves, that in the days of the Jews, thus lending out on interest was a sinful transaction, and, as such, condemned,
forbidden ; and if increase at all was forbidden, we must conclude that
the law was aimed equally at the respectable and reasonable Jew, who
took his six per cent, as at the exhorbitant one who took his hundred.
Quotations from a few passages of Scripture will, we trust, satisfy you
that lending on usury was entirely forbidden at least to the Jews ; and
even if the subject were involved in darkness and doubt, and we were
unable in our own minds, to comprehend the why and the wherefore of
this enaction, it would be wise on our part to obey the divine rule, and
meekly to say—" Even so Lord, for so it seemed good in thy sight."
But we trust we shall be able to show you that the thing is productive of
no good, but only evil and that continually, and that it must therefore in
itself be morally wrong—that it is in short, the fruitful source of all our
present commercial troubles.   Other evils may affect the financial world
—this from its universality, controls it with an iron hand   The removal
of this "ancient land mark" has opened the flood gates of an universal
deluge.

   The earliest intimation which we have of this law, is in Exodus
XXII. ver. 25 : " If thou lend money to any of my people that is poor by
thee, thou shalt not be to him as an usurer, neither shalt thou lay upon
him usury." This beautiful law of the purest charity is further elucidated
in Deuteronomy XV. ver. 7 and 8 : " If there be among you a poor man
of one of thy brethren within any of thy gates, in thy land which the
Lord thy God giveth thee, thou shalt not harden thy heart, nor shut thy
hand to thy brother ; but thou shalt open thy hand wide unto him, and
shalt surely lend him sufficient for his need, in that which he wanteth."
And again verse eleventh : " For the poor shall never cease out of thy
land ; therefore I command thee saying, thou shalt open thy hand wide
unto thy brother, to the poor and to the needy, with bread."   The New
Testament version of the same law is from the pen of the beloved disci-
ple, 1st John, III. ver. 17 : " Whoso hath this world's goods, and seeth his
brother have need, and shutteth up his bowels of compassion from him,
how dwells the love of God in him ?"   Thus we see that God comman-
ded that nothing should be lent on usury to the poor.   In Deuteronomy
XXIII. ver. 19, we find the same law includes rich as well as poor :
" *Thou shalt not lend upon usury to thy brother* ; usury of money,
usury of victuals, usury of anything that lent upon usury.   Unto a stran-

ger thou mayest lend upon usury, *but unto thy brother thou shalt not lend upon usury*; that the Lord thy God may bless thee in all that thou settest thy hand unto in the land whither thou goest to possess it." Here is the law in its widest and most comprehensive sense; usury, or increase or interest of any kind, strictly forbidden to be taken from any one, with a promise of a full blessing for the due observance of that law. We need not here stay to enquire into the exception made in regard to lending on usury to a stranger. Suffice it to say that He who employed the Israelites as His ministers of vengeance on the heathen nations of Canaan, thus relaxing, humanly speaking, the sixth commandment, might, in the same manner, relax the law of usury. Let us never forget that now, all men are brethren—that, if the command to Israel was, "root the heathen out of my land"—that of Christ is, "preach the gospel to every creature." It will be perceived that usury of victuals, and all other goods, was forbidden as well as usury of money; and all of you must be aware of the sad effects, in mortgaged farms, and poverty-stricken households, of the work of the usurer in many of the rural portions of this Province, especially amongst our Canadian brethren. They have presented a ready and profitable mark to the greedy and extortionate capitalist; and the dire effects are too obvious to be disputed. This is what the Bible means, when it charges the rich with having "ground the faces of the poor." These men could never survive "a year of release," and happy may they be that their lot is cast in such easy going times as ours.

In Leviticus XXV. verse 35, occurs this passage: "And if thy brother be waxen poor and fallen in decay with thee, then thou shalt release him: yea, though he be a stranger or a sojourner, that he may live with thee. *Take thou no usury of him, or increase*: but fear thy God, that thy brother may live with thee. *Thou shalt not give him thy money upon usury, nor lend him thy victuals for increase.*" These passages, it will be perceived, were mostly addressed to the rich, just because the rich were those most likely, through possession of means, to transgress this law, and the above quotation plainly shews to us the mind of God in the matter, that he considers usury to be the oppression of the poor and needy, and that, whenever it was exercised, it would be impossible for the poor to live in the land contented and happy.

In Proverbs, we find usury or interest classed with unjust gain, chapter XXVIII. verse 8: "He that by usury and unjust gain increaseth his substance, shall gather it for him that will pity the poor." Here is a threatening to deter men from that way which is abomination in the sight of God. Those who get gain by such means, however lawful and respectable they may appear, their riches will take wings, and their wealth will be transferred into the hands of merciful men who will pity the poor —a threatening too often fulfilled in our midst; for how many thousands have we seen, as in a moment, stripped of their wealth, and, in a manner, left destitute, or at least brought to stations far beneath those which they appeared formerly to occupy.

There can be no doubt our Saviour had the usurer in his eye, when he said, Luke VI. verse 34 : "And if ye lend to those of whom ye hope to receive, what thank have ye ? for sinners also lend to sinners to receive as much again."

Let us hear what the word of the Lord says in Ezekiel XVIII, verse 5th: "But if a man be just and do that which is lawful and right," verse 7th : " And hath not oppressed any, but hath restored to the debtor his pledge, hath spoiled none by violence, hath given his bread to the hungry, and hath covered the naked with a garment, *he that hath not given forth upon usury, neither hath taken any increase,* that hath withdrawn his hand from iniquity, hath executed true judgment between man and man, hath walked in my statutes and hath kept my judgements to • deal truly ; he is just, he shall surely live, saith the Lord God." Mark here the perfect man and behold the upright. Listen to the opposite view, verse 12th: " He that hath oppressed the poor and needy, hath spoiled by violence, hath not restored the pledge and hath lifted up his eyes to the idols, hath committed abomination, *hath given forth upon usury, and hath taken increase,* shall he then live ? he shall not live ; he hath done all these abominations, he shall surely die, his blood shall be upon him." What is to be said of our banks and banking institutions after such language as this ? What apology shall we make for our money borrowers and our money lenders after such a declaration as this ? What is to be said on behalf of our widows' funds, our orphans' funds and our church funds ? Did we ever expect to hear of such respectable corporations being classed among the abominations of the earth ? Turn a page or two of the same prophet, and you will find the character formerly drawn placed beside the shedder of blood and the extortioner—chapter XXII, verse 12th: " In thee have they taken gifts to shed blood: *thou hast taken usury and increase,* and thou hast greedily gained of thy neighbors by extortion, and hast forgotten me, saith the Lord God." And will any one tell me, that these plain words of Ezekiel were not intended for our day? Of one thing I am certain—there is nothing about ceremonial observances here.

In the fifth chapter of Nehemiah there is narrated a remarkable account of the afflictions suffered by many of the Jews through the borrowing of money, and the consequent mortgage of their lands and vineyards at the time of the re-building of the wall of Jerusalem. Acting under the godly advice of Nehemiah, the nobles and rulers under the oath of their priests, fully and freely restored, according to the divine law of remission, the mortgaged lands, vineyards, oliveyards and houses; also the money, corn, wine and oil, exacted of their brethren.

In Jeremiah XV. verse 10, we find the prophet, whilst, lamenting his sad state, saying: " I have neither lent on usury, nor men have lent to me on usury, yet every one of them doth curse me."

Let us hear in what language the Royàl Psalmist describes the man who shall abide in God's tabernacle, who shall dwell in his holy hill :— " He that walketh uprightly, and worketh righteousness, and speaketh the truth in his heart ; he that backbiteth not with his tongue, nor doeth evil to his neighbor, nor taketh up a reproach against his neighbor ; in whose eyes a vile person is contemned, but he honoreth them that fear thé Lord ; he that sweareth to his own heart and changeth not; *he that putteth not out his money to usury,* nor taketh reward against the innocent ; he that doeth these things shall never be moved."—Psalm XV. ver. 2 to 5. And will any one tell me that the book of Psalms was not intended for our day? Is not the law of the Lord perfect, converting the soul? Are not the judgments of the Lord true and righteous altogether?

I have thus quoted some portions of Scripture which shew us, in a clear and forcible manner, the mind and will of God with regard to usury. Of their meaning there can be no doubt—of their application I think there can be as little. The language is at once concise and explicit. Severe threatenings are denounced against those who transgress these laws; rich rewards are promised to those who keep them. So hateful must the usurer appear in the sight of God, that we find his doings classed with the most flagrant sins. Well does it become us daily to examine our ways, for so completely are our hearts blinded and corrupted, that we do not know how easily and smoothly we may be drawn into sin, nor how difficult it is, when once involved, to re-trace our steps.

Let us now examine into some of the results which flow from the system of lending money on usury or interest.

1st.—It gives a fictitious value to property of every kind, to all the inter-changeable commodities of life. The merchant who, without ready cash of his own, goes and begs from his banker a supply, whether he pay six, or twelve, or twenty per cent for the money, must, in order to enable him to compete and hold his ground with his neighbors, add a similar per centage to the value of the goods he sells. The intrinsic value of the goods, or that which is very properly regulated by demand and supply, is thus at once changed from a real to a false or apparent one, because the selling price is made to depend upon a fortuitous circumstance, namely, the inability of the merchant to buy except upon borrowed money. A tax of probably not less than 25 per cent is thus laid upon most of the articles of daily consumption. In many cases, it depends upon the merchant's standing and position, whether or not he can obtain money at a particular rate. Some have to pay double the rate of others ; another fortuitous ingredient is therefore introduced, and uncertainty is the result. The Hebrew law provided that the vineyards should not be sown with divers seeds, and that garments of various texture, such as woollen and linen combined, should not be woven. Here was a law to provide against adulteration, or the fictitious quality of goods ; and we all know to what an enormous evil this has now grown amongst us. And was it not just as likely that God should warn his people against a fictitious value as a fictitious quality, by prohibiting usury one with another.

2d.—It introduces an element of insecurity, uncalled for and unnecessary, into our commercial transactions. That insecurity is the rule, not the exception, facts abundantly testify ; and it will ever be so, as long as people trade on their neighbors' means instead of their own. In fact we cannot expect people to be so careful and circumspect with the means of others as with their own. The law of grace is, " as ye would that men should do to you, do ye also to them likewise" ; but the practice of this world has been appositely expressed in the well known proverb, " charity begins at home."

3d.—As it introduces an element of insecurity, so it also introduces one of uncertainty. How can any man who borrows money on usury, whether it be for three months or for three years, be absolutely certain of being able to re-pay it ? How often have we seen one of those innumerable accidents to which in this life we are ever liable, arrest in a moment all our plans, and sweep from beneath us those foundations on which we fondly hoped we were building a firm superstructure? And as in the day of battle the same confidence can never be placed on the mere mercenary soldier as on him who fights for his own hearth and home, so the man who trusts in his "bank advance" can never be sure how soon his discounts may be reduced or withdrawn, or how soon he may incur the suspicion or displeasure of those who have it in their power to inflict a fatal injury. Rest assured, the only safe man is he who fights his own battle.

4th.—Usury is the fruitful source of nearly all the commercial failures which we witness. This is a truth so self-evident that we hardly need require to waste words upon it. If every man would be content to trade on his own means alone, it would be practically impossible for him to become a bankrupt; for if he did lose his means, he would only be losing what belongs to himself, and no man would have the power to call him to account; and moreover, he would not, in his fall, be the means of dragging others along with him. Bankrupts and bankruptcy laws, with all their evils of oppression, fraud, expense and suffering would be at once and for ever swept from the earth. And if the civilized world, and especially the British nation, has made so great progress and extended its commerce throughout the earth, what does it show but God's blessing bestowed upon that commerce with all its attendant evils. Well may we, therefore, anticipate that time when a richer blessing on a better system will enable each man to sit under his own vine and fig tree with none to make him afraid.

5th.—As the Bible condemns the taking of usury, so experience teaches us that those who neither submit to it, nor practise it, are on the safest road. Tell me, who is the best customer?—the credit man, or the cash man?

6th.—The system of usury, as conducted by our Banks and similar institutions, opens a door for the encouragement of idleness. How many thousands invest their money for the purpose of being again lent out on usury, in order that they may throw the onus of its management on others, and thus lead easy, idle and quiet lives, not remembering that God sent them into the world to work whilst the day lasts, "seeing the night cometh when no man can work," nor that this "retiring from business," as it is called, is a thing forbidden by the word of God; that if "any should not work, neither should he eat." I do not believe that God ever bestowed more than enough of this world's goods upon any one of the children of men, or that the possessor of millions has not as much to do with it as the possessor of thousands. Every individual, and every piece of money has a certain and separate influence in the world; there is use for all. Whatsoever our hands find to do, whether it be matters of business or works and labor of love and charity, let us do it with all our might. The idle man, the " retired man," has no place in the creation of God.

7th.—The usurer tempts mankind to become discontented with his lot. This perhaps is at the bottom of the whole evil. All mankind are, with few exceptions, born into the world in the same condition, endowed with the same physical and mental faculties. The exceptions are the lame, the blind, the imbecile, the deaf or the dumb—living objects sent amongst us by God to excite at once our humility and compassionate regard. And if any grown man, possessing none of these bodily or mental infirmities, but in the vigorous use of his own reflecting mind and strong right arm, shall tell me that he never could have "got along" without the help of his banker or usurer, I will plainly tell him that I do not believe him. Here is the secret:—When a young man, perhaps just out of his apprenticeship, he wished to commence business for himself; but he had no means, or if he had, he did not deem them sufficient. He had perhaps squandered or lived up to his income; but he would not be " content with his lot," he must begin for himself and let the world see that he is somebody. If he has been a " fast young man" and wasted his living, he will not now become an economist. If he considers that with the utmost care he has not yet saved enough, he will not wait patiently till he has more ; no, he must begin now. He therefore, one way or another, succeeds in getting a " credit at the bank," and begins life on another man's money. He is now raised to the dignity of a merchant, and takes his three months bills, fondly hoping—just what all the world hoped before him—that he has thus carried himself forward a three months stage. If he succeed, well and good; if he goes down, it will only be what has happened to thousands before him, and his tarnished honour, and broken hopes, and vain repinings, will only be so much more added to the wrecks which cover the cold dead sea of commercial recklessness and ruin. We know too well that this is just the very way in which most of the community begin business—that on the very threshold of life, our young man places himself under an unnecessary obligation to others—places himself in another's power—spreads a net for his own feet—that his very first act is the act of a beggar ! Shew me, if it be possible, where is the dignity or self-respect here ?

8th.—If it be true, as I have endeavored to prove in my fourth proposition, that without usurers or usury there would be no bankrupts or bankruptcy, then we may justly charge that system with all those innumerable evils and disasters which we see resulting from such a crisis of commercial distress as we are now experiencing, not the least of which is the lamentable suffering introduced into the dwellings of the poor—that " great cry," as Nehemiah so strikingly expresses it, of " the people and of their wives against their brethren." It may be a matter trying enough to people's feelings, when they are unable to meet their notes or their just debts ; how much more sorrowful must it be, think ye, for a tender and compassionate father and mother to hear their offspring cry in vain for bread ? In short, the system is productive of evil, only evil, and that continually. Precious time is wasted by it—time which ought to be bestowed upon better objects. I do not know what proportion of every day it takes to arrange the payment of notes alone. I suppose just now it must be a very considerable part. The simple affair of a purchase and sale, instead of being there and then settled at once and for ever, is, by the means now used, a protracted matter, in many cases extending over an indefinite period, and is the source of infinite trouble and annoyance. Confusion and disorder are its unfailing results. The Babel which reared its head on Shinar's Plain, is not the only one which this world has seen.

We need not at present further pursue our enquiries into the evil effects of our commercial policy. Many others, I have no doubt, besides those I have just stated, will occur to your minds. I need not here refer to the gigantic system of swindling and fraud connected with the history of railroads, and which has too often turned what should be a positive blessing into a positive curse—to the absurdities and follies of many of our legal enactments, which have made the huge folios of our statute books, costly though they have been, a mighty fund of useless lore, and fit fuel only for the fire—to the chicanery and corruption of our courts of law, when too often justice is but a name, and right a shadow—or to the enormous evils of our Governmental system, which in this Canada is likely, as in the days of Nehemiah and the Jews, to place all our property under mortgages which we shall never be able to redeem. Do these things not all show us that our social system is rotten and corrupt to its very core ? May we not well exclaim " what shall the end of these things be ?" Well would it be for us and for our country, indeed, if the Mosaic law, in all its comprehensive simplicity and beauty, was made the statute book of the land.

There is one effect, however, of the usury system to which, more than all the rest, I would desire to draw your attention. It robs God—yes, robs him of his " tithes and offerings," of those means which ought to be dedicated to the " use of his temple." The startling question put by the prophet Malachi, " Will a man rob God ?" may justly be put in our days ; for the great bulk of mankind still seek their own, not the things which are Christ's. A stop is put to the circulation and preaching of the word of God among the heathen nations of the earth in times of such commercial convulsion as we now witness. The last and greatest command of our Saviour : "go ye into all the world and preach the gospel to every creature," has thus a practical arrest pnt upon it by the evil effects of a pernicious system, and although it may be the very last thing to which the minds of the community may be directed, or perhaps not directed at all, yet the alarming fact still remains that God is robbed, and robbed of that on which we know his heart is greatly set, the conversion of the heathen world to the kingdom of his Son. If such splendid triumphs with such limited means have attended missionary enterprise, might we not justly look for the subjection of the whole world to Him whose inheritance it is, were a divine law to regulate all our dealings in matters of money and property, and a sympathising heart to open a " wide hand" to our " poor brethren ?" Let us all, if convinced of the rectitude of a particular course, act up to that course as much as in our power. Every consideration ought to induce us to reflect upon our ways and doings. If we are to be taken to account for every idle word uttered, we shall also be called to account for every penny mis-spent. The influences arising from every word, and act, and thought, originating in time, stretch forward to eternity—small in their beginning, they are mighty in their results. The sun which shall tomorrow morning

" Pillow his chin upon an orient wave,"

will not find the world the same as he left it this night. The words of the speaker this evening—the thoughts of his hearers—will excercise an influence on generations yet unborn. Ought not such a momentous consideration as this induce us to be careful how our various means are acquired and spent ? Let us ever bear in mind that piety is a nation's strongest bulwark—righteousness the brightest jewel in her crown.

If I am not trespassing too much upon your patience, I would fain address a few words to my young friends. I speak unto you, young men, " because ye are strong." It is to you that the world looks for any great advancement, or for any social reform. Age, whether in men or manners, ought always to procure for it a certain veneration and respect. For you this was written :—"Rise up before the hoary head and honor the face of the old man." It is a beautiful sight to see the youthful mind taking instruction from the matured experience of age; and when such instruction is in accordance with divine revelation, the sun of old age sets indeed in unclouded beauty. Its path then becomes "like the shining light which shineth more and more unto the perfect day." Whilst it ought thus to be at once a pleasure and a duty to give "honor to whom honor is due," it is also a truth which young men ought never to forget, that the longer we continue in any particular course, the more naturally will our hearts incline to that way, whether it be good or evil. If an evil one, and persevered in, then that course will be like Pharoah's, both in its hardening process and its destructive end. It is for this very reason that I address you, young men. We may naturally consider that those who are advanced in years, have all arrived at their "fair havens;" they have had their day, and their work is done. But young men have yet a work to do. They are just embarking on the troubled sea of life, and cross it they must, one way or other. A great work is committed to the youth of this generation. The combined influences of six thousand years have descended, like a precious entail, to you; and it is for you to consider how best they can be used for your own and the world's good. For you, Mount Sinai still rolls its thunders on the echoing ear of time—for you the " still small voice" of Horeb's Mount still floats upon the air—for you, King David yet tuned his golden harp—for you, Mary yet sings Magnificat, and Bethlehem's shepherds listen to the angels' song. The great PAST hath committed to your care, young men, the Magna Charta of its rights and duties—see that ye pass it on unimpaired, with the additional herald of another good name to the eternal FUTURE ! The past sends down the stream of time to you, young men, a goodly ship laden with every thing glorious and precious— see that ye help to guide her on her way ! The past bequeaths to you, young men, a mighty chart to pilot you across the sea of life—a chart traced with many a curious line and intricate shore, but accompanied with a key which will tell you where the trade winds most do blow, and warn you of the sunken shoals where many a noble ship went down. This key is the Bible, the best of pilots, the surest and safest guide, and the careful study of which alone, can enable you to estimate every thing at its proper worth. This will be a result of inestimable value to you in all the affairs of life. There is no duty so trifling, no want so unimportant but may well deserve our earnest thoughts. Had the tear which dimmed the eye of the three months child by Nile's old wave refused to flow, a world's hope would have been perilled, a world's salvation might have been lost. Ponder then, I entreat you, what I have said to you this evening. Subtle minds, skilled in arguments, will endeavor to deceive you—expediency will tempt you to stray—inducements will be held out to you on every side—the world will tell you that to be rich is the end of life, and not to be over particular about the way. But make the Bible the rule of your life. Try all ways, and all arguments, and all expedients, by that unfailing standard; and, if they will not stand that test, then, in God's name let them fall.

I will bring this address to a close by a few remarks on the influence and use of money. Dr. Harris, in his prize work, "The Great Commission," says:—"The material itself, indeed, of which money is made, is intrinsically worthless; yet, having by the general consent of society, been constituted the representative of all property, and as such the key to all the avenues of worldly enjoyment, it excites some of the strongest desires, and reflects some of the deepest emotions of the human breast. Its fluctuations are the tides of national fortune. It sways the heart of the world. Every piece of coin that passes through our hand, has been streaming with influence from the first moment it was put into circulation. It hath a path through society and a history of its own; rather it belongs to the history of the world. Industry has toiled for it; enterprise has hazarded life for it; speculation has gambled for it; childhood has eyed it; poverty rejoiced over it; covetousness worshipped it it; hath passed through the hands of profligacy, intemperance and all the vices." To these forcible words we can hardly add. If its influence is thus universal, the evils resulting from the false or misdirected application of that influence must be universal too. Well, therefore, is its "love" or its inordinate desire said to be the "root of all evil." It is the great golden idol which is worshipped by this present age. So desirous are mankind to add field to field and house to house—to increase their wealth on every side— to wax richer and richer, that the beautiful precepts of gospel benevolence and charity are altogether lost sight of, or only awaken when some unusual calamity occurs in our midst; and then, in such a case, we are carefully advertised of every separate amount which charity bestows. And if the love of money is the root or source from which so much evil springs, so its proper and legitimate use is a means of good which sets all human calculation at defiance. How gracefully does the mantle of charity rest upon the good man who daily acts up to the important truth, "It is more blessed to give than to recieve," and in conformity with the injunction, " When thou doest alms, let not thy left hand know what thy right hand doeth." If money is not worth giving, it is certainly not worth having. Whatever differences of rank, wealth or intelligence we may see in this world, goodness is the only radical characteristic I can recognise. These, death will disrobe us of at the portals of the grave ; that will accompany us to a brighter and better shore.

Charity is the sure mark of a benevolent heart, benevolence the sure test of a charitable spirit. Ancient records abundantly prove that a time of usury and exaction was ever a time of poverty and distress ; present appearances show conclusively that the reign of the usurer has not yet come to an end. An usurious disposition and a hard heart go ever hand in hand. Usury holds its revel in a time of panic and distress. Usury shuts its hand upon the poor, hides its face from the needy. Usury, in its long and oft-repeated exactions, hardens the heart like the nether millstone. Usury built a Newgate for the poor debtor after it had made him such, and caged him there like a felon, till his latest breath. Usury robs you of your childhood's home, of your father's house, of your father's land. Usury piles burden upon burden on you, till you are left as it were without a hope. Usury robs the fatherless of their patrimony, and the widow of her right. Usury hath chased the smile from the face of childhood—it hath expressed from the eye of the mother the bitter tear—it hath traced the lines of premature sorrow, suffering and old age, on the brow of the strong man—it hath filled many an untimely grave ! Usury hath tied the hands of the diligent ; it hath strengthened the hands of the wicked. Usury hath made many children fatherless and left many widows mourning. Usury hath loaded the British nation with a debt which fools proclaim to be her strength, but the end of which wise men may not presume to see. Usury hath made this fair world one scene of desolation, suffering and woe. Will mankind not join with me in hissing such a system from the earth ?

SECOND LECTURE.

DELIVERED 4th Feb. 1858.—ROLLO CAMPBELL, Esq. IN THE CHAIR.

I think it will become me, by way of preface to my second lecture on the Commercial Crisis, to make you my acknowledgments for the kindness and courtesy with which you listened to the first. However deeply interesting to me, it would be a matter of no moment to you, to be informed of the circumstances which led me to direct my thoughts to the subject. Let me say that when I read my first lecture, I had no thoughts of ever reading a second. Many arguments having been brought against my views, some of them from the public press, I considered that I could not do otherwise than again venture before you to endeavor, if possible, not only to meet those arguments, but further to elucidate and strengthen my own ; and here I must also acknowledge the uniform courtesy which I have received from my opponents, so much so, that not one acrimonious word has been passed between us. I have desired only, if possible, to do some little good in our community, and if I have felt compelled, in addressing you, to say some hard things, ascribe all errors, if you please, to the head and not to the heart.

My last lecture has had just about the effects which I anticipated. It is in the nature of things that great truths and important principles should be long kept in swaddling bands. The orb of day, in his meridian brightness, casts a glory over hill and dale, but as he approaches the eastern horizon, the sober grey of morn first heralds the dawn, and as he declines beneath the western wave, the " glimmering landscape" gradually fades from view. Carefully must we tend, and patiently must we watch, the development of the plant which is at last to produce a flower to refresh us with its fragrance and please us with its beauty. The world is always slow to make social revolutions for the better. The things which have been intertwined with our earliest thoughts naturally adhere to us in our riper years, and we are unwilling to believe that practices which we have always followed, and which we have seen pursued unquestioned in the same manner by all around us, can be any thing else but right and proper. That the principles which I have advanced will ultimately prevail, I have not the slightest doubt ; for they rest on the broad and firm platform of the word of God. I am not one of those who believe in a secular education, or that any thing we learn, whether in the school or the workshop, the home or the market place, can ever be disconnected from religion. Every thing has a religious aspect, and nothing, therefore, can be purely secular. Had I not found, first and foremost, abundant reason in the word of God, I should certainly have hesitated to have advanced my views before you as I have done ; and, even had I deemed it desirable, it would have been found impossible to disconnect this subject from religion. The bent of my inclinations, the lessons of the Bible, and the nature of the subject, will, I trust, be sufficient explanation why I have presented it before you in the manner I have done.

Some there are who consider that because I have thrown a gauntlet before this community on the subject of usury, I should therefore be ready to meet every champion who appears against me, let him choose whatever subject he may ; that because I have declared usury to be sinful and too often the road to ruin, I must therefore be ready to tell how it came to pass that the Jews borrowed the gold and silver from the Egyptians when they were driven out of Egypt, and forgot to return them ; or to try to reconcile such disputants' ideas of right and wrong, with God's driving out the poor unoffending heathens of Canaan before the Jewish nation, and infefting that nation without pay or purchase, into the inheritance of another's labor. I should not here have taken notice of such things as these, had it not been too apparent that there are many who appear to shut out the light of day, because that light does not penetrate into every hole and corner. Now I beseech you, my friends, when you have mounted your steed, to bring him at once to the charge ; for if you persist in scouring through the whole theological field in this erratic manner, we shall never succeed in getting a thrust at you at all. There will always be probabilities and possibilities, matters of opinion and matters of faith.

The first object which I will take notice of is a common one, and that which is perhaps most frequently resorted to by those who differ from me ; at least, I find that when other arguments fail, this one is fled to as a forlorn hope or last resource. It is this :—That the laws given to the Jews on the subject of usury were intended for them alone—for a people placed in peculiar circumstances—and were never intended to apply to the present day and generation. The *Montreal Witness*—a periodical for which I have the greatest respect—in reviewing my last lecture, says: "The law against usury among the Jews was for a people placed in very peculiar circumstances; but it would not be wise to apply all their laws to nations as now constituted, and which occupy a very different position." Now I think this a very gratuitous sort of assertion; and were it carried out to its legitimate result, the *Witness* itself would be astonished at the fruit it would bear. It has quite surprised me to find to what extent loose and lax notions prevail regarding the ancient and venerable law of God. It was my privilege, a few Sabbaths since, to hear from a pulpit in this city, some remarks bearing on this very subject; and the reverend gentleman proved to us in the clearest manner that the moral law as given to the Jews, was not only binding on mankind to latest times, but was also binding on the many generations who lived and died before its promulgation from what is now one of earth's hallowed spots; and if the ceremonial law, or even the punishments which followed the transgression of some of the moral laws, have been abolished by the Gospel, these facts did not interfere in the slightest degree with the binding nature of those moral laws on all consciences. The *Witness* has not explained to us what the "peculiar circumstances" were to which he refers. If he means to say that the Jews were peculiar in having been constituted the first repositories of God's law, then I ask are we not a peculiar people too? Has that law in all its length and breadth and height and depth, not been committed to us too? "Shall our unbelief make the law of God of none effect?" Nay, let God be true and every man a liar. If the Jews and Gentiles are all under sin, they must be also all under the law, for by the law is the knowledge of sin. Does the *Witness* urge, "they were a peculiar people in respect that they were not, like us, a commercial people." I will answer that they were a trading people just the same as ourselves; they had their workers in iron, and workers in brass, herdsmen and ploughmen, soldiers and sailors, merchants and mechanics, just as we have now-a-days. They had gold and silver in such abundance, that, at certain periods of their history, silver was nothing accounted of—their shields and targets were of beaten gold. They traded by means of ships, with far-off lands—it is thought, even with that country which constitutes now our Indian Empire. I do not know if they could show such a piece of work as our Victoria Bridge, or the Leviathan steamship; but I am sure the seventy thousand carriers, and the forty thousand hewers, must have gone through a pretty good day's work. But the argument lies in a nut shell. If, as I think, the *Witness* refers to the Jewish people as placed in peculiar circumstances with regard to trade, is it not plain, that the difference, in that respect, between the Jews and nations as now constituted, is one only of degree and not of kind? and that the law which forbids usury may as justly be addressed to the dealer in pence as the dealer in pounds, to the lender of hundreds as to the lender of thousands? If you urge that the Jews were greatly addicted to usurious exactions, I will retort that a "Jew" is by no means a rare character amongst the British people. On this part of the subject, there can be but one argument of any weight You must prove that the divine law against usury propounded on so many occasions, and accompanied with so many warnings and threatenings, has been abrogated or done away with. Until ycu can show me that this law has in reality been done away with, we are bound to obey its dictates. There can be no doubt that it is a " law"—there can be as little doubt that it is a " moral law," for there is nothing ceremonial about it; and it was at first promulgated, with dread solemnity, from Sinai's mount. This sin has its origin in covetousness, and therefore it is a part of the ten commandments, and as binding in its obligations as " thou shalt have no other Gods before me." I have been able to reduce all arguments which I have heard on this head to a money expediency, and that a very doubtful one. There were no " peculiar circumstances" at all calling for such a law as this, other than that covetousness and corruption—that desire to be rich—that love of money—which is so deeply planted in every human breast. I trust I will be able to produce such a body of evidence respecting the effects of usury, as will lead you to the only conclusion that a tree which bears such fruits, must be a bad one; and I cannot see why this thing should not, like all others, be judged by cause and effect. Although many pretend to believe so, I cannot think that any part of the divine law can ever be an indifferent matter. That one example in the 15th Psalm where usury is associated with so much wickedness, and contrasted with so much righteousness, should be sufficient to settle the matter in the mind of every Christian and reasonable man. The wedge will be found there too firmly fixed ever to be removed. Until it can be shown that He who pronounced the law of usury binding on the Jews has relaxed its obligations on the Gentiles, or that its natural effects are good instead of evil, it surely would be true wisdom to obey the precept and not question the authority. The whole moral law, as given to the Jews, forms the most perfect and complete rule of life and manners which the world has ever seen or ever will see, and it is certainly a humiliating and painful sight to see that glorious law so openly repudiated as it is.

I quote again from the *Witness* — "We cannot agree with the lecturer in his views of taking interest. Money is a marketable commodity like flour or merchandise ; and if a man prefers to sell money, or the use of it, for a particular time, why should he not have a profit on it, as the storekeeper or farmer has on his goods or produce." Now I differ here entirely from the *Witness* and will endeavor to show you that money is not a " marketable commodity," and cannot be bought or sold like " goods or produce." Money, or in other words, the good gold and silver which constitutes the metallic currency of all civilized countries, there cannot be a doubt, has been intended by Omnipotent wisdom to be used as the great medium of exchange. In remote and rude times, many different articles were made use of as a money commodity, such as corn, cattle, cowrie shells, skins, and such like. But gold and silver, more especially the former, are the only articles hitherto discovered which possess in an eminent degree, the various qualities suitable in a medium of exchange. They are rare and costly, " good gear in little bulk," as the saying has it. They are easily fused and coined, are almost indestructible, and easily transported. They preserve their beauty untarnished for ages. Like other good things, the more we keep the dollar moving, the brighter it becomes; and its value is proved by the fact that the great heart of the world beats in sympathy with its rise and fall. Great labor is necessary in procuring this gold and silver. They must be dug from the mine or searched out of the sand, and the man who thus labors for and sells them in their rude state, or in any other state, to the goldsmith, the silversmith, the banker, the merchant, or the government, has as much right to be paid for his labor, as the farmer has to be paid for his grain, or the manufacturer for his cloth. Here it is only a simple commercial transaction, a buying and selling. The miller who sells his barrel of flour for five or six dollars, sells what he has labored for, and he considers that he has received in the five or six dollars, a fair equivalent for its value. The flour is not now his ; it belongs to the buyer.

The money is not now the buyer's; it belongs to the seller. If it has been an honest transaction, the miller cannot reclaim the flour, neither can the merchant reclaim the money. The flour is the merchant's, because it is paid for; the dollars are the miller's, because he has given value for them. A real transaction has taken place, a real exchange been effected. This is what I conceive to be buying and selling, and no one can deny that it is. But how, on this principle, can you buy and sell money? If you need one hundred pounds of money to-day, how much will you give for it? Why, is it not just worth one hundred pounds? and who is going to be so foolish as to exchange a shilling for a shilling, a pound for a pound? There is absurdity on the very face of it, and the two contracting parties would be justly considered two arrant fools. Is it not as plain to you then, as words can possibly make it, that money is not what the *Witness* calls it, a "marketable commodity, like flour or merchandise," and that this so-called buying and selling of money, is nothing else than borrowing and lending of it—very different things indeed, and which never can be identified one with the other. "But," adds the *Witness*, "a man sells the use of his money for a particular time." Now, if money be a marketable commodity like flour, as the *Witness* states, is it not rather a rich idea that of selling the *use* of a barrel of flour instead of the barrel of flour itself? We come then to the inevitable conclusion, that money cannot be bought or sold, like goods, but can only be transferred by borrowing and lending on usury—or, if you will have it—*buying* it " on time." If you voluntarily place yourself in a position which will require you to raise one hundred pounds to-day, to meet the wants of to-morrow, you will get it only after it has submitted to a shave from the keen razor of usury. Ah! this buying of bank notes, of good solid gold and silver, with your thirty or sixty days " promises" or intentions, is but an uncertain piece of traffic, too often uncertainty trusting to contingency, the dark future paying for the bright present. We are all intending, no doubt, to do great things—to become rich one day or other—and a strange world it would be, if all our hopes and anticipations were realised. Never is the truthful proverb, "there is many a slip between the cup and the lip," oftener fulfilled, than in the innumerable " slips" occurring between the drawing of a note and its maturity; and how often do our hopes, like many of those paper promises, prove but the " baseless fabric of a vision." Sufficient for the day is the evil thereof, without any uncalled for and unnecessary help from you to augment its calamities. If the borrowing and lending of the present age are identical with those of Scripture, I am afraid an "unauthorised" version has been palmed off upon us; for we all learn there that borrowing and lending are invariably such as *charity* can give, and *want* accept of, and that our speculating way of doing the thing is not only unauthorised, but strictly forbidden.

Let me again refer to the *Witness*. He says: "There is an advantage in many cases in lending on interest. Many possessors of money have no business qualifications, whilst oft times the men who have the latter have not the money. One of the former class may either enter into partnership with the business man, and make a profit on money in this way, or he may lend his money at interest and make a profit without going into business, for which he may be unfitted. In such a case, and it is not an uncommon one, the money is made useful to both men." Now this statement that many possessors of money have no business qualifications is a piece of mere gratuitous assumption, unsupported by fact; and you know facts are stubborn things. Are not the dealers in money proverbially accounted the keenest of men? Does not the case of the Western Bank of Scotland, of Strahan Paul and Bates, and of hundreds of others (for I presume that we only hear of the very disgraceful cases) plainly prove to us that the money too often gets into the hands of those who possess very doubtful "business qualifications" indeed, and that it would have been far better in the hands of the poor innocent people possessed of "no business qualifications" to whom it really belonged? Unfortunately, these people's qualifications leaned all the wrong way. In such cases, the money, instead of being made "useful," becomes destructive to both parties. But even though it be admitted that the existence of usury occasionally benefits certain individuals in a pecuniary point of view, this is no argument against our views on usury; for all laws are general in their application, and there are few of them which, although enacted for the good of society as a whole, do not apparently prejudice the interests of individuals.

But the statement that many possessors of money have no "business qualifications," I have already fully discussed in my first lecture. I take human nature just as I find it, and that is, pretty sharp in looking after the pounds, shillings and pence; and instead of finding many with no business qualifications, I think we may truly say that all are fitted just for their respective spheres, and that this presumption of no qualifications, is but a hypocritical mask under which idleness, if nothing worse, may conceal its features ; and he who thinks that he can thus fly in the face of divine commands so plainly revealed, by clothing himself in the garb of " no qualifications," is certainly doing a very foolish and wicked thing. One thing I am sure of, that this idea would not pass current with the bank shareholders themselves ; for, when a manager or cashier—although personally as upright as man can be—becomes the unconscious victim of wicked and designing men, these very shareholders are not only loudest in their declamations, but foremost with their cures. In view of the lamentable sufferings which have resulted in Britain from the recent disgraceful proceedings, I will not be astonished if for the future, less of the means of the aged and infirm are locked up, or rather dispersed and lost in the monied institutions. The young and the vigorous can begin life anew, but alas ! for the aged and childless sufferers, if they are cast upon a cold world's charity. The man who would advise them thus to commit their means to the care of heartless strangers, is taking upon him, indeed, a dreadful responsibility. If the storm has swept less lightly over Canada, let us not attribute it to a system rotten and corrupt, but to the goodness of Him who rules over all, and seeth not as men seeth.

I need hardly refer to the concluding argument of the *Witness* in support of the credit system, of buying £20,000 worth of goods with £10,000. The *Witness* has so well and so frequently argued out the advantages of the cash system, that I will content myself with simply turning his own weapons against himself ; and I subscribe, heart and soul, to the sentiment he uttered some twelve months since :—" If you go on for a week wihout pay, you may for the same reason go on for two weeks, or a month, or a year" ; also, to that on the 20th January last :— " When a paper is published on credit, every subscriber must pay something to make up for bad debts"—the very sentiment I uttered in the first proposition of my first lecture.

I confess I have been a little surprised at the arguments brought against my views, by one of our leading periodicals. Good anglers know that the smallest fish only are caught in the shallowest part of the stream, and so they should not be afraid to wet their boots. I regret that the profound and solid reasoning which the *Witness* has on so many occasions displayed, has not been brought to bear on this highly important subject. It is true, however, that the reasoning of the *Witness* is just what has been so often brought against me by many others.

It has been argued that it cannot possibly be wrong to do what all the world does and approves of. I do not mean to affront the intelligence of this audience, by making this opinion a point of special pleading. I merely notice it here to evince my belief that much of its danger consists in the universality of this sin. We are all so much accustomed to slide down this hill, that we cannot think it otherwise than a very good and smooth road. But may we not here profitably call to reflection, that in every conscience there is rooted " a tree of the knowledge of good and evil ?"

There is another objection which I will dispose of in a very few words, viz. that " usury has been generally considered to refer to what is called an *exorbitant exaction.*" But apart from the declaration of Scripture, which forbids increase at all, either in lending money, victuals, or goods, the whole course of argument I .have adopted, if it proves anything, proves that one per cent is condemned as well as one hundred per cent ; and I have taken care accordingly to frame these arguments upon the divine standard, that any increase at all on borrowed money is wrong. The only words employed in the Hebrew Scripture to denote usury, are —BITING, VEXATION, OPPRESSION.

It has been urged by some whose opinions are entitled to the highest respect, that the cause of the commercial troubles is to be found in the expensive style of living and dress which now so largely prevails. In so far as these are aggravations of the evil, such arguments are no doubt correct. I am told that one-fourth of the amount of importation of dry goods into New York during the past year, or that preceding, has been for expensive and unnecessary articles of female dress. Viewing the thing in a moral light, this of course is an evil, simply on the ground of Christian duty, because we ought to dispense with things unnecessary until needful things are provided. But if these showy trappings are bought and paid for, I do not see that in a commercial sense, we have much reason to complain. I am afraid the speculations of gentlemen exercise a far mightier influence than the haberdashery of ladies. It has also been acutely observed that there are too many merchants and too few farmers now-a-days. I believe, also, that there is some truth here, because agriculture is perhaps the surest basis of all prosperity, and there can be no safer bank for the investment of our means than mother earth, and our daily bread is the first necessary thing. But this evil, if it really exists, will find its cure in the demand and supply. There can be no doubt that the great disideratum, is *real productive industry*, less speculation, and less gambling.

Some have sheltered themselves under the exception made in Deu-teronomy in favor of the Jews lending money on usury to the stranger, or in other words, to the heathen nations around them. I do not see how this exception, even admitting it still to be in force, can be applied to us in the present day, for we all lend on usury to one another. With regard to lending to the stranger, the words are "thou *mayest* lend"; with regard to lending to the brother, the words are "thou *shalt not* lend." In the one case permission is granted, in the other the thing is positively forbidden. But all men now are brethren, for Christ has done away with all territorial and national distinctions; and if there was benefit de-rived by Israel of old in the prohibition of usury, we cannot doubt but that now, the Gospel intends that benefit to be conferred on all men— that as Israel, for so many thousand years, alone enjoyed so many privi-leges, so those privileges are extended with more ample blessings to those nations from whom all "disabilities" are now removed, and will be still fur-ther extended from day to day until a divine theocracy rules all mankind, and a goodly vine fills all the earth. I should think the very meaning and natural force of the word usury, "oppress," "vex," is a sufficient answer to this objection. The command runs thus : "Thou mayest oppress, vex, the stranger—the Gentile; but thou shalt not oppress, vex, thy brother." *Usury is oppression*—that is the Scripture view of it.

Reference has been repeatedly made to the well known and beautiful parable of the talents conferred on the three servants by their Lord; and exception has accordingly been taken to the truth of my views from the words in Matthew XXV. ver. 27: "Thou oughtest therefore to have put my money to the exchangers, and then at my coming I should have received mine own with usury." Our Saviour, in this parable, although he uses the words *money, talents* and *usury*, to illustrate his remarks, and to bring his instructions, therefore, more completely within the range of human apprehension, intends to teach, by these things, that we all have had committed to our care a vast amount of responsibility, and va-rious endowments, both of mind and body, and for the proper use of which we will one day have to give Him a substantial and particular account. But it does not, therefore, necessarily follow that our Saviour approv-ingly commended the practice of usury, condemned as it is in the Old Testament; for we might just as reasonably conclude that it ought to be our rule of hire to give no more to him who has borne the burden and heat of the day, than to him who has only worked one hour; or that our Saviour commended the unjust steward in his repeated acts of dishonesty; or that he approved the act of the unjust judge, who feared not God nor regarded man; or that, in the vision of the descending vessel which contained all manner of wild beasts and creeping things, Peter would have been justified, thereby, in eating all manner of abominable flesh. I know this parable has proved a stumbling block in the way of many. I do not think the matter can possibly be put in a plainer light; and it would be just as absurd to imagine that our Saviour commends such practices as these, as to believe that he commends usury; for he takes the one merely in illustration, as he takes the others.

The last objection which I will notice is the one which gives me the least concern. It is urged that these views can never possibly be carried out. This objection proceeds on the assumption that I have proved the truth of the opinions I have advanced. The truth I am willing to leave in the hands of those who believe it. Time only will prove whether or not they can be successfully carried into practice. All usury or interest was at one time strictly forbidden by the laws of England. Such was the case in the reign of Edward VI. and for hundreds of years previous to the reign of Henry VIII. In the reign of James I. of Scotland, there was a statute passed fixing the maximum rate of interest at 8 per cent, with this reservation :—" That this statute shall not be construed or expounded to allow the practice of usury *in point of religion or conscience.*" There is something exceedingly amusing in this provision; and these old legislators, whatever their practice had been, evidently understood the nature of the divine prohibition even better than Dr. Paley, who quotes this statute in his work on Moral and Political Philosophy. Our modern legislators take a more comprehensive view of things now-a-days, and do not attempt to present their views to us in such an interesting manner as the statesmen in the time of the first James; and so, to reconcile expediency with morality, they ignore the divine statute altogether. Verily, there are strange ways of getting conscience laid. The very fact that all civilised nations have found it necessary to pass restrictive laws regarding usury, proves beyond a doubt that there is evil in it, in the same manner as restrictive laws on the sale of alcoholic liquors evidences a public sense of its evil and dangerous character. This is one of the very arguments adopted by the advocates of tee-totalism, and there is a perfect parellel in this respect between the license law which is undoubtedly the main support of the traffic in intoxicating drinks, and the law establishing legal rates of interest on borrowed money. These laws came at last to be repealed, simply because they offered no check to the taking of usury. Perhaps no legislative enactment can ever be successfully applied in a question such as this. The matter is one which must be left to conscience—a far more powerful operator than Acts of Parliament. When once people begin to see that it is really the root of so much trouble, the counter of the usurer will be deserted —the tables of the money dealer overturned. There are some sins far beyond the reach of any restrictive law. There is but one legislative enactment which will reach a case of this kind, but a certain and a sure one—the voice of conscience—an enactment based on a sure foundation, even the principles of truth. We will see no fruit here, until we succeed in grafting the moral principle on the minds of the community.

When a merchant thinks that he sees a speculation which is likely to turn out very profitable, he will be tempted to give a large rate of interest rather than be without the money to carry out his views. There are other times, again, when a man will give almost any rate to save his note from being dishonored. In times similar to those we have recently experienced, I believe the most exorbitant demands must be submitted to in order to stave off the evil day, and no doubt many a comparatively honest tradesmen goes down, and suffers all the sorrow and ignominy of bankruptcy, while some accidental circumstance, if not some actual fraud, carries his more culpable and successful neighbor through with flying colors. Although there are mutual dependencies in nature, yet there are also individual responsibilities. If there are some things around us from which we all derive certain equal advantages, there are other tickets, which, in their very nature, have been stamped "not transferrable;" and those who give out their money on usury, and thus fly in the very face of God's command, requiring him, as plainly as words can speak it, to reverse his own decisions, may find to their cost, as many have found during the past six months, that there is a "wheel within a wheel," and that the revolutions of that wheel may present to them a startling and altogether unexpected phase. There are some risks certain and inseparable from life ; there are others purely of our own making ; and men's evil ways make this a strangely inconsistent world. There is no surer promise than this—that honest industry will meet with its due reward. On the doctrine of reproduc-

tive influence, no act or thought of man can be permanently lost; and
if it be true in the moral world that one good thought will produce
other good thoughts—a moral aphorism which, I think, cannot be disputed—so it is also true in the natural or material world, that labor or
industry, begun and carried on in an honest and proper manner, will not
only meet with an immediate reward, in a certain return corresponding
to the amount of diligence or labor bestowed, but will be the means,
however much unexpected on our part, of bringing in additional unlooked
for returns. Although we may be unable to explain, satisfactorily, how
this process is brought about, it only serves to prove that an unseen
hand is ever regulating, like clock-work, all the movements and influences of this lower world.

There is a class amongst us who hold, I suppose, a certain station and
influence in the commercial world, familiarly known by the name of
"shavers." I have had some difficulty, however, in arriving at the true
definition of a shaver. People seem to have different ideas of this
character, although, from his name, we take him to be one of the "lewd
fellows of the baser sort." Some will tell you that all exaction above
a certain rate, is shaving; but as wisdom is not measured by length of
beard, so, curiously enough, I find that money shaving is not always
measured by the amount of exaction; for some have declared that if
there was no legal rate of interest, there would be no shaving at all.
Barbers we know, and beards we know; but who is this shaver? And
then we hear of all sorts of shaves. We have the graceful, easy going
shave at six per cent, so quickly and so smoothly done, that it is hardly
felt. We have the rougher sort of shave at twenty per cent; and no
wonder if a tear some times follows such a rude shave as that. Then
we have the *stunner* of a shave at fifty or one hundred per cent. This
last shave will do the thing so completely, that, when you survey yourselves after the process, you will hardly recognise your own features.
In fact, you will begin to think, on your way back to your warehouse or
counting-room, that this wicked shaver might just as well have given a
cut lower, and finished the job at once. If you are at a loss to tell where
this trade begins and where it ends, this much I may say to you, that
his trade is *shaving fools*; and on his sign-board should be written:
"fools shaved here at all rates." Yes, my friends, these men will
plumb your necessities as they would do the deep sea. Their keen eye,
in which the blessed light of a tender sympathy seldom or never shines,

will fathom at a glance your crushing necessities, and pressing wants, and anxious cares. They carry with them a graduated line, fitted for every depth of human misery and woe ; and we need not wonder at the thrill of gratification which goes through the community, when we hear of a shaver being shaved !

Now we know that a shaver, as he is called, is a character held in universal detestation by the whole mercantile community. I confess I am at a loss to discern by what scale his iniquity is to be measured or estimated, or to see any mighty difference, in point of fact or morality, between the respectable usurer who leads a young man to begin business on borrowed money at six per cent, and the exorbitant money lender, as he is called, who charges, in a case of desperate necessity, one hundred per cent. Why, the extortioner is only acting on the same principle which guides insurance offices every day ; and is only charging, as McCulloch, in his Essays on Interest and Exchange, innocently but instructively calls it, " a premium of insurance for the additional risk he runs." You would pronounce it folly were an insurer to take the risk of a shingle-covered wooden house in a dense locality, at the same premium as he would a substantial tin-roofed store mansion in an isolated one. So it would be nothing less than folly for the dealer in money to shave you at the bank rate after the bank had turned you out of doors. If it is an admitted principle in trade to buy in the cheapest and sell in the dearest market, why should a different principle regulate this buying and selling of money ? And we invariably find those are loudest in their declamation of the shaver, who have had to submit to his hands. If there were none requiring to be shaved, there would soon be no shavers amongst us, and they would be compelled to seek other uses for their money. So would it not be better to beware of the first step which may lead you to have to submit to such a necessity ? One half of the community lives by shaving the other half. If we look at the risks and losses of business as at present conducted, we may put its net profits at twenty per cent per annum, and I think, if anything, I am over-rating the amount. Half of this amount, at least, will go into the pockets of the usurer ; and we cannot look for any other result. People must live—although idle, they cannot starve ; and as long as we believe in shadows, so long will there be found plenty to prey upon our credulity.

Usury neither increases nor creates capital. If every usurious transaction were this moment brought to an end, there would not be a whit less cf real capital, or real industry, or real wealth, in the country. It is true we will always see riches and poverty—successful men and unsuccessful men—one getting up, another falling down—one community spreading itself like a green bay tree, and another dwindling away into utter insignificance. So true it is that the "lot is cast into the lap, but the disposal of it is from the Lord." But without industry there can be no real production or increase of wealth. The curse pronounced upon man, "in the sweat of thy face shalt thou eat bread," rests upon the world to this day, and shall rest upon it to the latest time. It is a very part of our nature, interwoven into all our being and existence, that without labor there can be no result.

How then can the mere act of lending a sum of money on usury create capital? or in other words, how can the discounting of ten thousand bills by any bank be the means of creating capital? It cannot be any thing else than the mere exchange or transference of capital from one to another. We do not deny that the banks increase or add to their capital, but we do most positively deny that they create any themselves; for it is only the mercantile community, the merchant, the mechanic, the farmer employing that capital in re-productive industry, who add to the material wealth of the community. So it may be said most truly of banks and all usurers, that they do indeed enter into other people's labor.* Even Shakespeare seems to have understood it in that light, for he speaks of usurers "taking a breed of barren metal." Let no man think that because he may happen to have been left in possession of wealth, he is entitled to invest it where he can at once get quit of the trouble of its management, and share in the real productive industry of another. How can an idle man like this be said to be obeying the divine command, "replenish the earth, and subdue it?" How can he be said to be diligent in business—to be earning his bread by the sweat of his brow? Working by proxy in this way will not do, for the account to be rendered at last will require to be a personal one. And on the other hand, let me warn young men, whatever be their rank in life or means of estate, of beginning the world on borrowed capital. It is far better

* "The present system of banking with debt is continually piling debt upon the people, and spreading bankruptcy and wretchedness over the land."—See an able article on Interest and Cheap Currency, by C. H. C., in the *Canadian Merchant's Magazine and Com. Review*, February, 1858.

† The banking system, politically or morally, *is nothing but evil*. The inevitable fate of all banks is only a question of time."—R. Sulley, in *Hunt's Mer. Mag.* for March, 1858.

surely to check the first risings of covetous desire, than to begin a course which may eventually lead you to dishonor and ruin. Let the foundation on which you build, be laid sure and deep. Take a lesson from the mighty structure which is now being erected to span the St. Lawrence at your doors. Let your house be founded on the rock, and then, when the rain descends, and the floods come, and the winds blow, your house will not, like the one without foundation, be dissolved amongst the sand. If your unlawful desires should be accomplished, and you should succeed in borrowing a sum on usury, either from a bank or an individual, you are taking what is not yours, what never was yours, and which may possibly never be yours. You are entering on a course which the Bible condemns, and which all experience forbids. You will tell me perhaps, that you give an equivalent for its use. Let us hear what that equivalent is. It is a piece of oblong paper called a " promissory note." That certainly costs little, and if we may judge from what we see, it is a sort of coin too easily manufactured and too credulously received. Oh, but, you say, we have something at the back of it. Well, let us hear what you have at the back of it. It is our goods, you will say. But are your goods paid for? If they are not, they are not yet yours. If they are paid for, they are paid for with another's money, with the proceeds of your first discounted bill, less the shave. But then you will say, the goods are in my store. But of what use are they there? Do we not see, every day, warehouses filled with goods, and the owners of them, aye, and real owners of them too, unable to raise a single cent upon them to meet current engagements? Oh, but you will perhaps add, the goods are sold, and I have a three months bill for them, and I must just go to my banker and get another discount. So you pay for the first note by the proceeds of your second, less again the shave. Now I may ask you, are you sure this note of your customer's will, after all, be paid? What if you should fall into the hands of designing and dishonest men, who will not only rob you, but glory in their shame? You cannot positively be certain that the note will be paid, and in this very uncertainty, constituted as human nature is, and coupled with the responsibility under which you have now placed yourself, rests in part the evil of the thing. You have, without the shadow of an excuse, created for yourself an unnecessary risk, and in such an important matter, too, as that of your business, and you have no right to complain if you smart for it. It may be all very well for those who are getting along swimmingly to scoff at this reasoning; but let the evil day only come upon them, and their scoffs will be turned into mourning, and they will begin to think that, after all, there was some truth in this reasoning. There are too many accommodation notes always in circulation; because, of course, some subterfuge must be had recourse to in order to fill the void occasioned by the disappearance of those things we had hoped were substantial and real; and the public have been too often gulled by the publication of " bogus' statements. I do not mean to say, that the majority of promissory notes are not, in good times, promptly and honorably met; but this I mean to say, that a system which, in its origin and commencement, is evil, must of necessity, sooner or later, submit to a purging process; and what have all our far-fetched schemes of financial improvements been, but complications of the evil? If we sow to the wind, we shall certainly reap the whirlwind. The longer the world lasts the faster it moves. The nearer we approach the centre of attraction, the greater the momentum of our speed. And so we see these commercial crises, in spite of all legislative enactment, coming upon us faster and faster and with increasing severity; and mankind will yet be compelled to look the evil in the face. The course of illustration and argument which I have adopted in these lectures, in laying bare the causes of the present crisis, has also, at the same time, made plain the cure. It would no doubt be considered a very fine thing, if some rich nabob were to come amongst us to-morrow, and, with princely generosity, liquidate all our debts. But that, for us, I conceive, wonld be a very questionable kind of generosity indeed, and would prove but a premium on further speculation and recklessness. However deeply we may be just now involved by the present commercial troubles, it never can be too late to retrace our steps. Let us but put on the moral resolution to work only on our own means, and although it may take five years, or ten years, to heal present diseases, yet every day after such a resolution is once formed and acted on, brings us a day nearer the desired consummation.

And then with regard to the period of maturity of a note, is there not positive absurdity in a system which will bring dishonor on you, if you are not within bank doors by a particular hour on the day it falls due? To-morrow would perhaps put all right, but to-morrow comes all too late. Red-tapeism has done its work effectually, and no plea can now avail. The stain is cast upon you—the Rubicon has been crossed; and of course they who make such promises for a certain day, are expected to provide for all contingencies. The mistake even of a date, may bring upon you a discredit which, perhaps, never can be wiped away.

Out of the facilities held forth by the usury system, has arisen the dangerous practice of suretyship, by means of which the simple minded and too confiding cautioner becomes surety for sums often beyond his means, and without even the usual consideration of " value received." I think you will all agree with me in condemning this practice; and all of us may endorse the language of Scripture with regard to it:—"He that is surety for a stranger shall smart for it; if thou be surety for thy friend, thou art snared with the words of thy mouth. Be not thou one of them that strike hands, or of them that are sureties for debts."

There is another circumstance which, in passing, I must briefly notice. Whilst a shaver may be mostly always found to listen to your proposal to take off your beard, however rough or long it may have grown, there are times when the banks, even in those communities where they are unrestricted by any legal enactment, will refuse to shave you at any rate, or for any inducement. Your beard has grown altogether too long or out of character or fashion, and it would turn the edge of their keenest razor to take off such a hirsute appendage as yours. No matter how old a customer you may be, or how often you have been respectably shaved there before, you can get shaved there no longer. And then, have not recent explosions on the other side of the water plainly shown, that too often the honest mechanic or tradesman has been denied a shave, whilst the bloated millionaire or capitalist, as he was vainly considered to be, has been pampered to such a degree, that his own weight has at last brought him down. Like the over-taxed boiler, the bubble at last bursts and spreads ruin and devastation on every side. Time went far too slowly for his expansive powers. Usury and speculation did their sure work. The gambler and his too confiding banker came down together; and it would not be a very great matter if their's were the only regrets we heard. But beneath all there comes forth a deep under-current of lamentation, and mourning, and woe. Surely such things as these will at last bring people to sober and calm reflection—will compel us, at least, to give such a system a few passing thoughts.

Usury is one of the principal causes of the great disparity which we see in the present day, between rich and poor. Not a penny is considered well spent, unless we see a certain return of additional

money capital in a certain and productive rate of interest. A common-
wealth is neither a healthy nor a wealthy one, where we see so much of
superabundant wealth and harrowing poverty. It is now an admitted
axiom in the political economy of our country, that the middle classes
of Great Britain are her real strength. The immense and unnaturally
distended landholding interests of England, Scotland and Ireland, I
would consider but very questionable elements of strength ; and that
policy a very doubtful one indeed, which leads the landed aristocracy of
the mother country—as we see it, more especially, now pretty fully
developed in the Highlands of Scotland—to banish the hardy peasantry
from their parent soil, and cause their expatriation to a foreign land.
Such men will never rest satisfied till they have turned their native country into a wilderness or a vast deer forest. When lately in the Highlands
of Scotland, I saw many instances in which far more care and consideration were bestowed upon the beasts that perish, than on him who is made
after the image of God. If ever there was a spot fitted to be the habi-
tation of man on earth, it is along the shores of the beautiful Loch Tay
in Perthshire ; and yet, round all its fair circuit of nearly forty miles,
money could not buy you as much land as would suffice to rest the sole
of your foot. Long may our free country be preserved from a worldly
minded and grasping aristocracy. And we may just make similar
statements with regard to a monied aristocracy. The public mind in
England has recently been confounded and shocked at the astonishing
disclosures of fraud, falsehood and dishonesty, connected with many of their
public institutions. The " merchant princes" have come down wonder-
fully of late, and what was their pride and their boast, has now become
their dishonor and their shame. People will yet be compelled to learn
that they may force business to an unnatural degree of extension—that
they may build a Leviathan which they may never be able to launch—
that the bright hopes with which they have anticipated an uncertain and
unknown future, may after all come to be disappointed—and that those
whose motto is the reverse of " live and let live,"—for whom the world's
surface would be all too small, and for whom all its wealth would not
prove sufficient, may yet come to endure not only the finger of scorn,
but the sufferings of want. It is impossible for any one to measure the
extent of human misery which must of necessity follow the breaking
down of one of these monster establishments. As sure as night succeeds
day, so sure is poverty increased and aggravated by such an occurrence.

F

Results prove that these great riches were not real—that they had no foundation, and existed only in appearance. Of what use is appearance without reality? Had these big men traded on their own means, they would not only have had certain and enduring riches, but they would have prevented certain and enduring poverty. Providence sometimes takes strong measures to compel us to look our errors in the face.

The work of the usurer, or lender of money on interest, is a *dishonorable* work. The very nature of the commodity in which he deals, and the manner in which that commodity is lent, conjoined with the uncertainty he feels whenever his hard cash is entrusted to you, necessitates him to keep a sharp look out on your ways and doings—to pry into your standing and position in society—into the amount of your property and means. And why should he not become a spy upon all your actions? Has he not a monied interest in your purchases and sales—in your profits and losses? Has he not sold you the *use* only of his money? Has he not a monied interest in the number and character of your servants—in the quality of your table—in the character of your family? Has he not a monied interest in your labours, and cares, and anxieties—in your risings early and sittings up late—in your very flesh and blood—aye, in your very life and death? Is he not entitled to enquire of your neighbour across the way how you are getting along? If you are under large advances, and some heavy loss or domestic calamity drive you to the debauch, has he not now an additional reason to be particularly anxious about you? A feeling of sympathy, we may fain hope, would be one of the motives to induce him to admonish you as a brother—a tender regard for his money, we may fear, will occupy the most of his thoughts. Has not the truth itself, in many cases, to be either garbled or concealed, for fear of giving offence in high quarters? What can be said, then, for such a system of espionage and tyranny?

Usury often becomes a dangerous instrument of tyranny and oppression. I need not enlarge on this head. You all know that the man who has vast sums of money at his disposal, has at his command means of no ordinary power.

The usurer who lends money on interest to the prodigal and the spendthrift, becomes a partaker of his sin. However startling such a statement as this may seem, yet common sense declares it to be unquestionably true. You would never count him a charitable man who relieved every beggar who importuned him. Such a man would exhibit folly without discrimination; and, in certain countries, he would find his purse empty before his charity had waxed warm. Such a man's charity could be considered only a premium on vice, wretchedness and rags. And yet, for my part, I cannot see any difference between the usurer who, whatever be the nature of the security offered, lends a spendthrift or prodigal a sum of money, and the gentleman with the misplaced and mistaken charity, who, without any prospect of return or increase, opens his hand to every bold beggar by the way. If there is any difference, it is in favor of the latter, for he gives hoping for no return, whereas the usurer not only puts the means in the hands of the prodigal, knowing him to be one, but takes care that he shall again receive his own with usury. And we need not here say how many a fair estate has helped to swell the profits and dividends of our monied institutions. No christian man would think for a moment of giving a drunkard intoxicating liquor. The possession of a thing cannot relieve us from the moral responsibilities attachable to its use. We must not cast a stumbling block in the way of the blind— we must not drive our horse and waggon furiously through a crowded street. Whatever be the results arising from such wrong ways, we are chargeable with the sinful cause. In short, the man who thus lends out his money on interest, is every whit as much a gambler as he who throws the dice; for both of them make but a speculation and a gamble of things they have no right to gamble with, and practically disannul God's word that he who does not work neither should he eat, and practically disbelieve His oft-repeated promise, that they who are diligent in good works shall not want for any good thing. It is a righteous thing that they who underwrite for the wild waves and the stormy winds, should suffer from these winds and waves. It is a righteous thing that they who underwrite for the burning fire, should suffer from the devouring flame. It is a righteous thing that they who dare to traffic in life and death, should suffer from life and death. And it is just as righteous a thing that they who trade in the risks and chances of the dark and unknown future, should suffer from that unknown future.

I do not mean any one to gather from these lectures, that I insist on a perfect equality of means, or that I believe in the communist theory. That utopian idea has arisen from a false consideration of the very constitution of human nature; and those who think that such notions (however social they may at first sight appear) will ever be introduced into human society, may as well think of binding the wind or arresting the whirlwind. One star differeth from another star in glory. There is a harmony which is beautiful—there is a sameness which is not desirable. There is a variety which pleases—there is a tameness which fatigues. As varied as the features of men, so varied are their intellectual and moral capacities; and so long as we see industry and sloth, economy and prodigality, so long shall we see to a certain extent the same appearances as at present exist in the distribution of the elements of wealth. We are not, however, on that account, to make life a juggle, nor labour a lottery. If there is a way of faith, there is also a rule of manners; and assuredly those rules which profess to ameliorate the condition of fallen humanity, and to restore it as far as possible in this uncertain life, to its original purity and beauty, are worthy at least of our attentive and serious consideration. "No man liveth to himself," is a truth worthy of being written on the front of every day-book and ledger in the city.

When a co-partnery is formed to carry on business, it is generally an understood thing that all parties engaged shall share equally in the profits and losses. Let us see how the case stands, or how this safe and reasonable rule applies in lending money on interest to a firm or individual for the purposes of trade. We find this rule will not work here at all. You borrow from a bank a certain sum, say for three or six months, to be invested in your business. That sum you must repay at the stated period, with a profit of six per cent, or whatever the rate may be ; or rather, the profit is generally deducted from the money before it begins to move —before you have touched a single farthing of it, or before that money has earned any return. Now, the bank, or party from whom you have borrowed this money, although they claim a share of the profits, will not share in a single penny of the losses. These losses may be heavy, but the bank must be repaid in full. It is true your banker cannot demand more from you than the stipulated rate of interest ; but this, on reflection, you will easily perceive, is just another phase of the case as absurd as the one we are considering. Now, we wish to enquire upon what grounds the lender shares only in the profits of the borrower. He can only urge, that it is because he has the money, and runs a risk in lending it. But, I may ask, has the lender any more risk in lending it, than the borrower has in trading with it ? If the one commits it to an uncertainty, so does the other. And has not the lender often a far greater amount of security for his money, than the trader has for his? But then, you say, the lender lends his money which is his own, and which he has, by his industry, accumulated for himself, to ne who has no means. **Now,** setting aside the question of security, may I not justly ask here—is it true that the borrower has no means? I contend that it is not true; and that we may fairly place his honesty, his integrity, his intelligence, his industry, in short, all his business qualifications, against the value or use of the other's money. And there is no body so quick at putting these things at their proper value, as the money dealers themselves. Put the two things in the balance, the mere money against honesty and industry, and tell me which scale will go down. I will await with some curiosity to see by what system of logic it can be made to appear that the lender of money for profits to be made in business, should not share in its losses likewise; and those who deliberately enter into such unequal contracts, cannot complain, if, as they so often do, they come out on the wrong side of the account.

Nature is a great teacher. If we begin to meditate upon that wonderful analogy which exists throughout the whole of the material world, we cannot for a moment doubt that God has designed that world to be a great instructor of man. It is a school-board on which are chalked truths suited for all intellects—lessons suited for all minds. It is a volume which teaches the rudiments of grammar, as well as the curiosities of literature. Well hath it been said that " the word of God and the works of God are the two great doors to the temple of truth." The most delightful teaching which ever fell upon the ear of man, has been derived from the lilly of the field, or the fowls of the air. Man is so constituted, and the world has been so framed, that one is but the counterpart of the other. The most important lessons obtrude themselves upon us at every step; and so palpable are they, that all may see them, if they will but open their eyes to them, and all may understand them, if they will but meditate upon them. The occurrences of one day, are but the lessons for the next—the events of the past, the guide for the future. I have somewhere read that the finest honey is often to be found in the slenderest reed, and so the sweetest kernels may sometimes be discovered within the hardest shells. Let us see then if we cannot discover, in the material world, some fitting illustration, bearing more immediately upon the subject of this lecture. We have not far to go. I will take one with which you are all familiar—the plain and humble bee-hive. Beneath the rough straw dome we will find an example of the most patient industry and unflagging zeal. Here is a community for you, which the busiest

of us all may take a lesson from.   Mark them how they are abroad at
earliest dawn —watch them throughout the live long hours,

> " Gathering their honey all the day
> From every opening flower,"

and see them returning, with the declining sun, laden with their honied
spoils.   Apply your ear to the hive when evening has drawn its shadows
around, and listen to their song of praise.   The harmonious hum of ten
thousand wings strikes on your listening ear.   These little fellows " covet
earnestly the best gifts."   Nothing but the finest honey from the flowers
of the field will satisfy their desires.   The blossoming bean field, and the
broad leaved lime, are alive all day long with their busy hum.

> " There as the wild bee murmurs on the wing,
> What peaceful dreams thy handmaid spirits bring."

There is no idleness here ; all are as busy as bees can be, and each fur-
nishes its share to the general store.   Architectural knowledge is won-
derfully displayed in the construction of their cells ; foresight and frugal-
ity in the industry which provides, and the economy which stores a supply
of winter's food.   There is, however, a jarring interest even here, which
at times wakes the little colony to arms.   This is the presence of those
bees known by the name of " drones."   It is certain that these drones
add nothing to the general stock, but exist only off the labors of the
working bees.   What their use is, or why they are there, has never yet
been ascertained.   Perhaps they were put there just to keep us in
mind that there are drones in our hive too.   I well tell you, however, what
is done with the drones.   When they begin to assume airs to themselves,
and become so numerous and so greedy as to threaten to eat up the winter stock, the working bees commence a simultaneous attack upon them,
and banish them from the hive.   You may see a drone—for they are well
fed powerful fellows—flying off with three or four workers hanging upon
him.   You may see them dragged out by main force to the entrance of
the hive, their wings dexterously cut at the point of insertion with the
body, and then—oh ! unlucky drones—tumbled headlong to the ground.
Here they soon perish ; for the working bees, you will perceive, do not,
like us, take half measures.   Or, if a drone should escape, and happen for
the moment to save his wings, it is really amusing to watch him alight
again on the hive, (for like some wise people, they will often come back
to be bitten) take a survey round and round, and then make a sudden dash

through the entrance on his back. But it is of no use—forth he is speedily dragged, and shares the fate of his fellows. Now, ladies and gentlemen, are there no drones in human society? Are there none eating up our
hard earned gains? And then, what is to be done with them? We
must go cautiously to work; for they are generally, you know, pretty fat
and heavy fellows, who would make rather a stout and stubborn resist-
ance. If we resort to force, they might probably make such a commotion as would bring the whole hive down about our ears. As I suppose you are all of mild dispositions, and averse to extreme measures,
perhaps the quietest way would be to give a clip here, and a cut there,
—in short, to withhold the supplies; and then the drones would either
be forced to work like the rest, or take their flight to other diggings.

There is one means of "raising the wind" too common amongst us, and
to which it may be profitable to direct a few thoughts. I refer to the
habit of getting money on the security of our dwelling-houses and lands.
The same reasons which I have adduced against borrowing on goods or
notes, may be applied here with additional force. The man who builds
for himself a house and home, finishes it, pays for it, and then, for the sake
of some imaginary profit in some imaginary speculation, places it under
a mortgage for borrowed money, may find that, instead of "raising
the wind," he has raised a whirlwind. The evil of this thing is aggravated by the consideration that the necessity for it exists only in the man's
imagination—that it is not real. He is called a heathen man who provides not for the wants of his household. Is he anything better who can
thus rob his family, perhaps, of a shelter from the cold winds of heaven? I
believe many good and honest men place themselves in situations like this,
only through a carelesness and want of thought. There would be less
danger if we only looked at the tree bearing its natural fruits. Is not
the Irish Encumbered Estates Court a great and important fact? And
are not these encumbered estates themselves, great and important facts
too? The history of mortgaged houses and farms may well be written in tears of blood; for the man who is greedy of gain will spread
his net anywhere and everywhere—. Sooner or later the wolf will come
to the door, and then fear will come as a desolation, and destruction as
a whirlwind. Why then should you place yourselves in the power of a
man who would "take thy bed from under thee, or the roof from over
thy head?" Let us all beware of making rash vows which we may never
be able to perform, or which others, to our sad experience, may perform

at our cost. "Home, sweet home." Our tenderest recollections cluster around that word ; and who amongst us can ever forget the hallowed memories of that sweet spot. We look back upon it as the one green bower in a waste and howling wilderness. How often, with sad and chastened thoughts, do we contemplate, in the dim vista of the past, this green isle of childhood's early day. How often will memory, from its clouded throne of three score years and ten, send back a ray of light through the intervening gloom of years, till it rests, like the swallow in its eaves, on that spot called *home*. How often will the aged man live o'er again his boyish days—will climb again his native hills, and revive and warm his time-dried limbs over the decaying embers of a fire which will flare and flicker to his latest breath. Like the subtle electric fluid, influences will come mysteriously down the track of time ; and sympathies, like golden beams, which the lapse of years cannot dim, nor the cold Atlantic wave ever quench, will flash back again from memory's faded shrine, till, longingly and lovingly, they rest upon the spot called *home*. Even as the setting sun, so often in this western land, leaves behind him a firmamental glory—a light o'er hill and dale—which no pencil can portray. Home is like the placid lake in an Indian sea, surrounded and defended by its coral reefs from the commotion and storms of the rude main beyond. And though these stormy waves may everlastingly rage and lash into foam against its rocky barrier, yet, upon its adamantine reefs, they will but sing their own requiem, and the still lake will ever calmly and sweetly smile. So around the inheritance of our fathers, God hath drawn a moral bulwark, which can never with impunity be broken down ; and how stern must be the necessity which ever impels ruin's ploughshare through such a fair scene ! How wicked and vain must that first act of covetousness be, which, in the long run may rob us of a spot like this, and turn those dear to us as our own blood, adrift upon the cold charity of the world ! It is peril, just the more imminent, because it is so often done and so lightly thought of ; and no man can be justified in entailing such a calamity upon his children. I am far from saying that there are not many noble hearted men and women amongst us ; but, as a general rule, let but unfortunate turns of business bring in the world upon you like a flood, the averted eye and the cold calculations of a worldly profit and loss will plainly tell you where that world's sympathies are too often to be found. That small yet cunning piece of mechanism, the human hand, will guide a Leviathen over the waves. The movement of one lever will put a complicated machinery in motion. So let us beware of the great fire which one mis-directed act may kindle. Farmers of Canada ! beware of land sharks—beware of land banks. Guard your farms and homes as you would your lives. They may prove a refuge to you in many times of trial. See that no burdens are placed upon them. Flee from mortgages. Never place your farms in death's hand.

I have lately had put into my hands a printed copy of a lecture by Mr. James Miller, entitled " Protest against the Corrupt Practices intro- duced by the Rechabites, Sons of Temperance, and others," delivered at Guelph, August 4th, 1857. I have read this pamphlet with no ordinary interest, and consider it the work of no ordinary mind. He has brought reasoning to the illustration of his views which it is impossible to gainsay, and has clothed his subject with a christian garb which entitles it to all respect. I merely notice Mr. Miller's Protest here, to recommend it to the careful perusal of those who, like myself, consider society in danger of becoming more and more corrupted by the spirit of gambling and speculation which now so largely prevails. Those who want to know what gambling, in its nature really is, and what its accursed effects inva- riably are, would do well to read and study Mr. Miller's Protest.

Nothing, probably, could have been found more effectually to lock the wheels of commerce, than the usury system. Were an arrest put this moment upon that system, would there be any valuable thing lost to the world—any essential ingredient which commerce could not want ? Would there be a penny of less capital to be circulated ? Would there be less real comfort amongst us ? Would there be any honest in- gredient lost ? Would labor be less productive ? Would industry be less active ? I will tell you what, on the contrary, would be the results. Speculation would receive its death blow. Credit—that mistaken and misnamed word—would exist no more as it exists now. The idle would be forced to work—the drones would be driven from the busy hive. The very locomotives, in their race of industry, would whistle forth a rejoicing song. Industry would ply its busy task in every street and lane. Com- fort would make a home of all our dwellings. Forests would be sooner felled ; land would be better cultivated ; and the very earth would yield a better increase. The wilderness would be made to rejoice and blossom as the rose. " Dunning" would come to an end. Poverty, like a frighted spectre, would take its departure. We would not see great capitalists, and bloated millionaires, luxuriating on the means of others, with crowds fawning on them at every step; but we would see honest merchants, and honest mechanics, working cheerfully with upright hearts and strong arms —all the more cheerfully directed, because they would no longer live in fear of the credidor's bill or the bailiff's charge. Customs and taxes would come so lightly upon us that they would be hardly felt. There would be less corruption in high places, just because there would be less opportunity. Buying and paying, selling and receiving, would be relative events. Forgery and fraud would be powerfully arrested. The earth would be sooner civilized, and an Indian mutiny, with all its horrors, become more and more a moral impossibility. Charity would then give with a liberal hand, just because, in giving, it would know that it was giving what was its own. Our houses would be built and paid for ; our churches would be built and paid for ; and our ministers would have their labors better paid for. Brother would not need to go to law with brother ; and our ears would not be shocked, as at present, with hearing of numbers of our fellow colonists languishing in a debtor's cell. There would be fewer heart-burnings and jealousies in families. The main stay and prop of the crowned despots of Europe would be broken, and tyranny fall prostrate to the earth ; for money has such a potent spell, that the want of it would seal up the cannon's mouth and lay the bayonet in the dust. Commercial crises would come to an end, and we would not be compelled, as now, to read in all the languages of Europe, over the tomb of the nations' commerce :—" This is ruin, and ruin's road." The lark singing at heaven's gate would then be a fitting emblem of that prosperity and happiness which would flow down our streets like a mighty stream.

I intended to have made some critical remarks here on *trade*—its nature and objects, its duties and responsibilities; but I find that the length to which this address has already extended, will deter me from entering upon the subject. I had intended, if possible, taking the Bible as my guide—for this and all other social questions must yet come to be worked out from the good old book—to show that the first announcement we have of trade or labor, was embodied in a curse pronounced by the Lord God upon man, and upon the ground for his sake—much in the same manner as the confounding of language and consequent dispersion throughout the earth followed hard upon the presumptuous thought of building a city and tower whose top would reach to heaven. Surely it cannot be thought an indifferent matter to endeavor to ascertain how that curse may be turned into a blessing, and how its disastrous effects can be most readily neutralized—the sweets of life made to mingle in its bitter cup. It is too obvious that the time has arrived when an absolute necessity exists for the enlightenment of the public mind on these things ; for the spirit of gain has long been feasting on forbidden fruit, and threatens every day to make still further advances on forbidden ground. To judge from statements shamelessly put forth, re-echoed on every side, and credulously received on every hand, it looks as if nothing would be restrained from this money-loving age which it imagines to do. It is, therefore, surely high time that such iniquity should be stripped of its mask, and its true features exposed to those who are too easily duped by its fair appearance.

I have thus, I think, in these two lectures, proved beyond the possibility of controversion, the existence of this law of usury, and its binding power upon all consciences. The purest benevolence towards our fallen race is exhibited in the institution of such a law. If it be true that " day unto day uttereth speech, and night unto night showeth knowledge," it must also be true that every day, as it dawns, brings with it, not only oft-repeated warnings, but multiplied and increased responsibilities ; and the more we hear and the more we learn, so are our responsibilities augmented in a corresponding degree. The voice which, long ages since, first spake to Cain :—" Where is Abel thy brother," is still wandering throughout this world, repeating the question over and over again to every man, seeking rest, as it were, and finding none. To you, therefore, who have heard all the words of this law, and without thought or consideration turn again to the " beggarly elements" of a worldly practice —I say that by this very law which ye think so lightly of, ye will be one day judged. To you who, on the other hand, may be bestowing upon it that reflection which its nature and authority so much demands, I can only repeat: " Be ye thoroughly convinced in your own mind." Those who do not like to retain this salutary law in their knowledge, may perhaps come to be given over to the vile affections of the covetous sin which it condemns, and then indeed the " gold will become dim, and the most pure gold be changed."

I need not here repeat the reasons which induced me, more particularly, to address young men in my last lecture. I know full well that it is a future, and perhaps yet distant generation, which will embody to any extent in its practice, the truth of the principles I have so feebly endeavored to advance and establish ; and I believe the world has yet a great deal to do and to suffer ere the time arrives when "glory shall dwell in our land." You, my young friends, are the heralds of that generation. You will bequeath to it, as from father to son, your own opinions and your own practices. Many of you are not yet committed to the ways of the present age, and are not yet involved in its troubles and perplexities. You have no lee way to make up ; you have no steps to retrace ; you have not yet lost your vantage ground. Consider, then, the words I have spoken to-night, as being more particularly directed to you. I feel desirous now to address a few parting remarks to you, on something of far more importance than the things which perish with the using. I shall come short of my desires if I succeed only in bringing you to reflect on worldly matters—on time without reference to eternity— on means without reference to an end. Somehow or other I feel impressed with the responsibility of the situation in which I have voluntarily placed myself ; and as it is not likely that I shall ever have such an opportunity again, I am desirous that my parting words may leave some permanent impression behind them. Recollect then, that you have all one great Creditor, to whom you are all indebted, whom you cannot defraud, and who will one day require from you his own with usury. The talents which He has committed to your care are various and numerous. Some of them are splendid talents indeed, comparable to fine gold. There is the talent of Reflection, by means of which we prove all things. Be not deceived by the maxims of the world—try them and see what they are made of. The delicate sieve of a reflecting mind, guided by the standard of God's holy word, will sift these maxims through and through, and as it parts with the offspring of the weed and the thistle, will preserve nothing but the precious grain. If on calm and sober reflection, you find these maxims to be good, then hold them fast, lay them up in the treasury of a faithful and believing heart—practise them in the daily business of an honest vocation. If on the contrary, you find these maxims nothing but chaff, then let the wind drive them away. And then there is the talent of Moral Firmness, which will enable you to hold fast the things proved to be good ; and this talent, put into the hands of Perseverance, will bring you safely through many a dark and troubled day. There are the talents of Benevolence and Generosity, twin sisters of the rarest beauty. Let these be kept ever active by a Love which recognises every man as a brother, and let all be guided by the hand of a wise Discrimination. There is the talent of Temperance, which, alas! is now so often hid in the earth.

But, on the other hand, there is a sin under which mostly all other sins may be classed—an in-born and all-prevailing sin, wide, broad and deep —the sin of *covetousness*, the " root of all evil." This sin will undermine and ruin the fairest structure; it will overtop and hide all good graces ; it blighted Paradise of old. " We brought nothing into this world, and it is certain we can carry nothing out," is a truth which, if rightly reflected upon, will cut the sin of covetousness to the quick· Lay not up then unnecessarily either for yourselves or a future generation. That generation will be amply provided for ; because summer and winter, seed time and harvest will never cease. Recollect that money is a thing to be kept in circulation, and not to be hoarded. It is one of the most precious material talents God has given us. Its value is so great, its means of doing good so unlimited, and the claims upon it so many and so pressing, that we are blameable, in a manner, if we allow a single shilling to remain idle for a single day. Therefore I would quote to the words of John Wesley :—" Make all you can—save all you can all you can." As I said before, make the Bible the rule of your life. Here is a bank for you which will never break down—a bank of deposit, and bank of issue. No means of notation that we have can ever estimate its capital. Its dividends are sure. It has a *rest* laid up for those who adhere to its rules and regulations, which will, as a bonus, be hereafter distributed to them with a liberal hand ; and its " promises to pay" are all secured in the records of Heaven by the word of Him who is the same yesterday, to-day, and for ever—endorsed by thousands of his saints who still walk this earth, and by the mighty cloud of witnesses who have gone before and are entered into that rest. Finally, have faith in God—the best talent of all, and which will brighten all the others. Then, when the last ministering angel comes to do his work, and ye have entered into the dark valley, ye shall emerge out of that valley into a land of beauty, compared with which, earth's fairest spot would be a wilderness —where gold and silver will be as plentiful as the stones in the streets of Jerusalem—where the talents which ye have so well used in this world, will be all returned to you again a hundred fold, with a " well done, good and faithful servant, enter thou into the joy of thy Lord."